TI
TROUBLES

CHITRA SOUNDAR
ILLUSTRATED BY HANNAH MARKS

BLOOMSBURY EDUCATION
LONDON OXFORD NEW YORK NEW DELHI SYDNEY

BLOOMSBURY EDUCATION
Bloomsbury Publishing Plc
50 Bedford Square, London, WC1B 3DP, UK
29 Earlsfort Terrace, Dublin 2, Ireland

BLOOMSBURY, BLOOMSBURY EDUCATION and the Diana logo
are trademarks of Bloomsbury Publishing Plc

First published in Great Britain in 2020 by Bloomsbury Publishing Plc

A catalogue record for this book is available from the British Library

ISBN: PB: 978-1-4729-7082-4; ePDF: 978-1-4729-7080-0; ePub: 978-1-4729-7081-7;
enhanced ePub: 978-1-4729-7079-4

2 4 6 8 10 9 7 5 3

Printed and bound in Great Britain by Bell and Bain Ltd, Glasgow

MIX
Paper from
responsible sources
FSC® C007785

All papers used by Bloomsbury Publishing Plc are natural, recyclable products from wood grown
in well managed forests and other controlled material.

To find out more about our authors and books visit www.bloomsbury.com
and sign up for our newsletters

Chapter One

It was nap time in the jungle. Sloth Bear wasn't sleepy. Whenever Bear wasn't sleepy, she got bored. Whenever she got bored, she looked for Porcupine.

But Porcupine was fast asleep, curled
up in a ball, on the next tree.
"Wake up!" called Bear. But Porcupine
didn't hear a thing.

Bear picked some guavas from her tree
and threw them at Porcupine.

Chapter Two

SPLAT!

The guava smashed and splattered all over Porcupine. He woke up startled. When startled, Porcupine always did what his mum had taught him.

DANGER! DANGER!
CURL FROM STRANGER!

He curled back into a ball and rolled down the tree.
TUMBLE, TUMBLE, THUD!
Oops! Porcupine fell on Crocodile's head as he rolled away.

OUCH!

Crocodile woke up in alarm. When alarmed, Crocodile always followed her mum's advice.

DANGER! DANGER! RACE FROM STRANGER!

The muddy riverbank was very slushy and slippery.

WHOOOSH!

SNAP!

Crocodile splashed as she fell into the river and snapped at Elephant's tail.

Chapter Three

AWWWWWWH!

Elephant hopped on three legs, hurt by the tug on his tail. When hurt, Elephant always did what his mum told him to do.

DANGER! DANGER! FLEE FROM STRANGER!

So he ran out of the water on to the banks. He ran helter-skelter, staggering all over the forest.

BUMPITY BUMP!

He ran into the guava tree. The tree shook left. And then it shook right.

Sloth Bear looked down, holding on to a branch with all her might. "Don't do that!" she cried from the tree. But it was too late.

DUMPITY-
DUMPITY-
DUMP!

10

Sloth Bear screeched loudly as she hurtled down the tree. But she did not fall on the hard ground. Neither did she fall into the big puddle under the tree. She fell on something soft, warm and scary.

Chapter Four

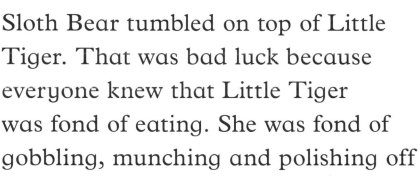

Sloth Bear tumbled on top of Little Tiger. That was bad luck because everyone knew that Little Tiger was fond of eating. She was fond of gobbling, munching and polishing off her food.

"Yum!" said Little Tiger. "Sloth bear salad is my favourite. I'm going to eat you up."

"Wait, wait," cried Bear. "It wasn't my fault. I was sitting on top of the tree, eating guavas. I fell on you because Elephant shook the tree."

Elephant trembled in fear from his trunk to his tail. But he didn't want to get Bear into trouble. So he came out of hiding from behind the trees.

"I shook the tree," moaned Elephant. "But it was an accident."

"Ooh!" said Little Tiger. "I love elephant éclairs. I'm going to eat you up."

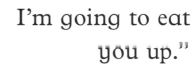

"Wait, wait," cried Elephant. "It wasn't my fault. I bumped into the tree because someone bit my tail."

Little Tiger thought about it for a moment.

Chapter Five

"Sloth Bear fell on me because Elephant shook the tree," said Little Tiger. "Elephant shook the tree because someone bit his tail."

"That's right," said Elephant and Bear.

"Who bit Elephant's tail?" asked Little Tiger.

Crocodile peeped out of the water. She didn't want to get Elephant into trouble. So she crawled onto the banks and whispered, "I bit Elephant's tail but it was an accident."

Little Tiger smacked her lips. "Crispy crocodile crackers are amazing," she said. "I'm going to eat you up."

"Wait, wait," said Crocodile. "It wasn't my fault. I bit Elephant's tail because someone knocked me on the head."

Little Tiger thought about it for a moment.

Chapter Six

"Sloth Bear fell on me because Elephant shook the tree," said Little Tiger. "Elephant shook the tree because Crocodile bit his tail. Crocodile bit his tail because someone knocked on her head."

"That's about right,"
said Bear, Elephant
and Crocodile.
"So who knocked
Crocodile on
the head?"

Porcupine unrolled himself and peeped
out from under the leaves. He didn't
want Crocodile to get into trouble.

"I knocked Crocodile on the head," he whispered. "But it was an accident."

Little Tiger growled. "Porcupine pizza, right at my doorstep," she said. "I'm going to eat you up."

"Wait, wait," cried Porcupine. "It wasn't my fault. I fell on Crocodile's head because someone threw sticky guavas at me."

Little Tiger thought about it for a moment.

Chapter Seven

"Sloth Bear fell on me because Elephant shook the tree. Elephant shook the tree because Crocodile bit his tail. Crocodile bit his tail because Porcupine fell on her head. And Porcupine fell on her head because someone threw guavas at him."

"That sounds just about right,"
said Bear, Elephant, Crocodile
and Porcupine.
"Who panicked Porcupine then?"
asked Little Tiger.
Everyone looked around. Who was it?

No one peeped out of the trees or scuttled out of the bushes. No one came to explain.

Sloth Bear gasped. She realised that she had started it all.

Chapter Eight

"About that," said Bear. "I wasn't sleepy and I wanted someone to play with. So I tried to wake up Porcupine by throwing guavas at his tree." Little Tiger thought about it for a moment.

"I'm not sleepy either," said Little Tiger. "Can we play together then?"

"Porcupine rolling, Crocodile running, Elephant bumping and my jumping has made me very tired," said Sloth Bear, with a big yawn. "I *am* sleepy now."

That made Porcupine yawn too and
then Crocodile did. Elephant yawned
right after. The yawn soon spread
through the forest like a bad smell.

Even Little Tiger yawned.
"Me too," she mumbled, walking
away to her den.
It was nap time in the jungle. Not
a leaf moved nor a creature stirred.

The sleepy
animals slept until
the jungle turned
dark and starlight
sparkled through
the leaves.